Dear Parent:
Your child's love of reading starts here!

Every child learns to read in a different way and at his or her own speed. You can help your young reader improve and become more confident by encouraging his or her own interests and abilities. You can also guide your child's spiritual development by reading stories with biblical values and Bible stories, like I Can Read! books published by Zonderkidz. From books your child reads with you to the first books he or she reads alone, there are I Can Read! books for every stage of reading:

 SHARED READING
Basic language, word repetition, and whimsical illustrations, ideal for sharing with your emergent reader.

 BEGINNING READING
Short sentences, familiar words, and simple concepts for children eager to read on their own.

 READING WITH HELP
Engaging stories, longer sentences, and language play for developing readers.

 READING ALONE
Complex plots, challenging vocabulary, and high-interest topics for the independent reader.

 ADVANCED READING
Short paragraphs, chapters, and exciting themes for the perfect bridge to chapter books.

I Can Read! books have introduced children to the joy of reading since 1957. Featuring award-winning authors and illustrators and a fabulous cast of beloved characters, I Can Read! books set the standard for beginning readers.

A lifetime of discovery begins with the magical words "I Can Read!"

Visit www.icanread.com for information on enriching your child's reading experience.
Visit www.zonderkidz.com for more Zonderkidz I Can Read! titles.

*"Give her any help she may need from
you, for she has been the benefactor
of many people..."*
—Romans 16:2

ZONDERKIDZ

The Berenstain Bears® Mama's Helpers
Copyright © 2011 by Berenstain Publishing, Inc.
Illustrations © 2011 by Berenstain Publishing, Inc.

Requests for information should be addressed to:
Zonderkidz, 3900 Sparks Drive SE, Grand Rapids, Michigan 49530

Library of Congress Cataloging-in-Publication Data

Berenstain, Jan, 1923–
    The Berenstain Bears' Mama's helpers / written by Jan and Mike Berenstain.
       p. cm. – (I can read. Level 1)
    ISBN 978-0310-72099-7 (softcover)
    [1. Housekeeping–Fiction. 2. Helpfulness–Fiction. 3. Bears–Fiction. 4. Christian
life–Fiction. I. Berenstain, Michael. II. The Berenstain Bears' Mama's helpers. III. Mama's
helpers.
    PZ7. B44826Bim 2011
    [E]–dc22
                              2010016485

Editor: Mary Hassinger
Art direction & design: Kris Nelson

Printed in China

17 18 19 20 21 DSC 15 14 13 12

The Berenstain Bears® MAMA'S HELPERS

Story and Pictures By
Jan and Mike Berenstain

Living Lights™

GOOD DEED SCOUTS

The Good Deed Scouts were up
bright and early.

They were having breakfast at
the Bear family's tree house.

"What shall our good deed be today?"

asked Scout Lizzy.

Scout Brother had an idea.

"Mama could use some help," he said.

"We will be Mama's helpers today,"

said Scout Sister.

"That will be our good deed."

"As the Bible says," pointed out Scout Fred,

"'honor your father and your mother.'"

"Good point, Fred," said Brother.

"Mama," said Sister,

"the Good Deed Scouts will be

your helpers today."

"That's nice," said Mama. "Start by

clearing the table, please."

"The Good Deed Scouts

at your service!" said the Scouts.

After the table was cleared,

there were other chores to do.

The Good Deed Scouts washed, dried,

and put away the dishes.

They washed the counters.

They swept up crumbs

from the kitchen floor.

"You are doing a good job," said Mama.

"Now let's go to the living room.

These rugs need to be cleaned."

The Scouts took the rugs outside.

They hung them up.

They beat them with a rug beater.

Clouds of dust came out.

Papa saw the clouds of dust.

He came to see what was going on.

"Are you burning leaves?" he asked.

"No!" said Brother, coughing.

"We are cleaning rugs."

"Here," said Papa. "Let me try."

Papa whacked the rugs.

Even bigger clouds of dust came out.

The dust drifted behind the tree house.

Mama was hanging out her clean wash.

"Oh, my goodness!" said Mama.

"My clean wash is getting dirty!"

She told Papa and the Scouts to stop.

"That's enough rug-beating," she said.

"I have other chores for the Scouts."

Mama sent the Scouts up to the attic.

"There are piles of papers up there,"

said Mama.

"Please tie them up.

Then bring them down to recycle."

The Scouts and Papa went to the attic.

The Scouts tied up the papers.

They knew recycling showed respect

for God's creation.

Papa found some old clothes in a

trunk and put them on.

He put an old record on a record player.

"I remember this old song," Papa said.

He danced around the attic.

Mama heard the music.

She came up to the attic.

"Hello, my dear," said Papa.

"May I have this dance?"

He danced around with Mama.

The Scouts all laughed.

"This is fun," said Mama.

"But chores need to be done."

"You are right," said Papa.

"I will get back to work too."

Papa went back
to his shop.
The Scouts carried the
papers downstairs for
recycling.

"Honey is getting cranky," said Mama.
"Please play with her."

So the Good Deed Scouts
played catch with Honey.

They played peekaboo and blocks.

The Scouts put on a puppet show

for Honey—

"Snow White and the Seven Bears."

Honey giggled and clapped.

Soon it was time for lunch.

Mama made a nice lunch

for the Good Deed Scouts.

"You are the best Mama's helpers

ever!" Mama said.

"Hooray!" said the Scouts.

"Another good deed done!"